RIPLEY'S
RBI
FACT OR FICTION?
BUREAU OF
INVESTIGATION

ISBN : 978-1-893951-59-4

10 9 8 7 6 5 4 3 2 1

Design: Dynamo Limited
Text: Kay Wilkins
Interior Artwork: Ailin Chambers

For information regarding permission,
write to VP Intellectual Property, Ripley Entertainment Inc.,
Suite 188, 7576 Kingspointe Parkway, Orlando, Florida 32819

Email: publishing@ripleys.com
www.ripleysrbi.com

Manufactured in Dallas, PA, United States
in October/2010 by Offset Paperback Manufacturers

1st printing

Trading card picture credits: b/l Zak-n-Wheezie hatched on 6/14/07 to Frank and Barbara Witte of www.fresnodragons.com

THE LOST ISLAND

a Jim Pattison Company

INTRODUCING THE RBI

Hidden away on a small island off the East Coast of the United States is Ripley High—a unique school for children who possess extraordinary talents.

Located in the former home of Robert Ripley—creator of the world-famous Ripley's Believe It or Not!—the school takes students who all share a secret. Although they look like you or me, they have amazing skills: the ability to conduct electricity, superhuman strength, or control over the weather—these are just a few of the talents the Ripley High School students possess.

The very best of these talented kids have been invited to join a top secret agency—Ripley's Bureau of Investigation: the RBI. This elite group operates from a hi-tech underground base hidden deep beneath the school. From here, the talented teen agents are sent on dangerous missions around the world, investigating sightings of fantastical creatures and strange occurrences. Join them on their incredible adventures as they seek out the weird and the wonderful, and try to separate fact from fiction ...

▶▶ RIPLEY

The Department of Unbelievable Lies

A mysterious rival agency determined to stop the RBI and discredit Ripley's by sabotaging the Ripley's database.

The spirit of Robert Ripley lives on in RIPLEY, a supercomputer that stores the database—all Ripley's bizarre collections, and information on all the artifacts and amazing discoveries made by the RBI. Featuring a fully interactive holographic Ripley as its interface, RIPLEY gives the agents info on their missions and sends them invaluable data on their R-phones.

THE TEACHERS

▶▶ Mr. Cain

The agents' favorite teacher, Mr. Cain, runs the RBI—under the guise of a Museum Club—and coordinates all the agents' missions.

▶▶ Dr. Maxwell

The only other teacher at the school who knows about the RBI. Dr. Maxwell equips the agents for their missions with cutting-edge gadgets from his lab.

MEET THE RBI TEAM

As well as having amazing talents, each of the seven members of the RBI has expert knowledge in their own individual fields of interest. All with different skills, the team supports each other at school and while out on missions, where the three most suitable agents are chosen for each case.

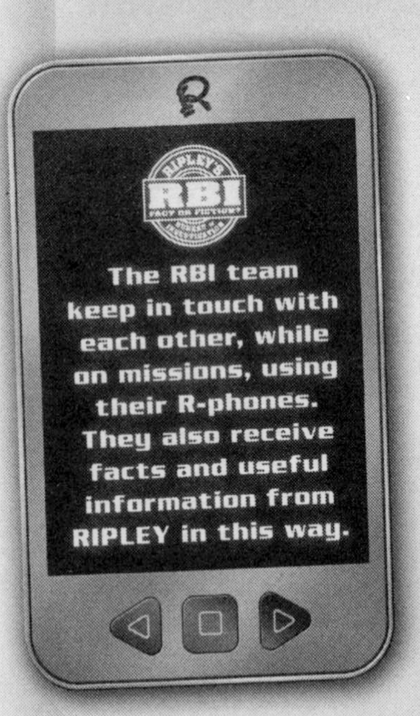

▶▶ KOBE

NAME : Kobe Shakur

AGE : 15

SKILLS : Excellent tracking and endurance skills, tribal knowledge, and telepathic abilities

NOTES : Kobe's parents grew up in different African tribes. Kobe has amazing tracking capabilities and is an expert on native cultures across the world. He can also tell the entire history of a person or object just by touching it.

ZIA

NAME : Zia Mendoza

AGE : 13

SKILLS : Possesses magnetic and electrical powers. Can predict the weather

NOTES : The only survivor of a tropical storm that destroyed her village when she was a baby. Zia doesn't yet fully understand her abilities but she can predict and sometimes control the weather. Her presence can also affect electrical equipment.

MAX

NAME : Max Johnson

AGE : 14

SKILLS : Computer genius and inventor

NOTES : Max, from Las Vegas, loves computer games and anything electrical. He spends most of his spare time inventing robots. Max hates school but he loves spending time helping Dr. Maxwell come up with new gadgets.

KATE

NAME : Kate Jones

AGE : 14

SKILLS : Computer-like memory, extremely clever, and ability to master languages in minutes

NOTES : Raised at Oxford University in England by her history professor and part-time archaeologist uncle. Kate memorized every book in the University library after reading them only once!

ALEK

NAME : Alek Filipov

AGE : 15

SKILL : Contortionist with amazing physical strength

NOTES : Alek is a member of the Russian under-16 Olympic gymnastics team and loves sports and competitions. He is much bigger than the other agents, and although he seems quiet and serious much of the time, he has a wicked sense of humor.

▶▶ LI

NAME : Li Yong

AGE : 15

SKILL : Musical genius with pitch-perfect hearing and the ability to mimic any sound

NOTES : Li grew up in a wealthy family in Beijing, China, and joined Ripley High later than the other RBI agents. She has a highly developed sense of hearing and can imitate any sound she hears.

▶▶ JACK

NAME : Jack Stevens

AGE : 14

SKILLS : Can "talk" to animals and has expert survival skills

NOTES : Jack grew up on an animal park in the Australian outback. He has always shared a strong bond with animals and can communicate with any creature—and loves to eat weird food!

BION ISLAND

SCHOOL

THE COMPASS

HELIPAD

GLASS HOUSE

MENAGERIE

GARDEN

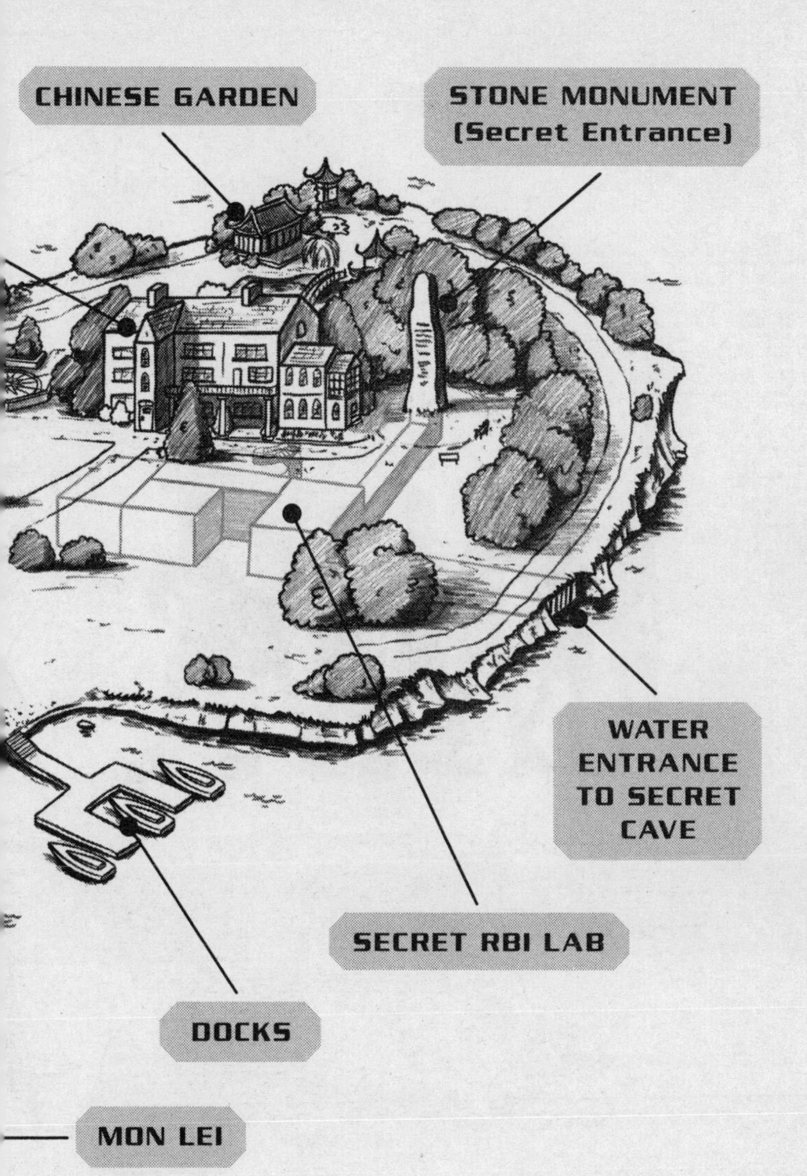
CHINESE GARDEN
STONE MONUMENT
(Secret Entrance)
WATER
ENTRANCE
TO SECRET
CAVE
SECRET RBI LAB
DOCKS
MON LEI

Prologue

The sun had not long been up and was gaining strength as it beamed down on a small village near the coast of Tanzania, in Africa. A young boy began his walk to the schoolhouse, as he did every day. He knew the way well and there was no reason for him to suspect that this morning's walk would be any different from the trip he took to school every morning; but for some reason he did. As he walked he listened to the sounds around him and noticed that something was different. The bird calls were not the same as every other day; something must have spooked them. The grass in the scrubland he walked through had been crushed, as if a herd of rhinos had run across it. Then, as he was studying the trampled ground, something caught his eye. He looked up in time to see a large shape rush out in front of him and stop for a moment before disappearing again behind a large bush. The boy dropped his school bag in shock, but then tried to calm himself. He rubbed his eyes, not quite believing what he had seen. At first glance it had appeared that the creature might have been an elephant; the boy quite often saw elephants not far from his village, so this would have been nothing unusual, but the creature

seemed to have been covered in thick reddish-brown fur. He had never seen a fur-covered elephant before. He moved toward the bush where the creature had disappeared, hoping to get another look, when a horrendous noise tore through the strangely quiet air. He covered his ears, quickly. The sound was like nothing he had heard before, it sounded pained and menacing at the same time and he was not sure he wanted to know what could have possibly made it. The boy stood still for a second, filled with fear and unsure what to do, but then the terrible noise came again and the bushes rustled as if the creature responsible might appear and head toward him. In his mind something that made such a ferocious noise would surely eat people! As the sound filled the air for a third time, the boy could take no more. He willed his feet to move and ran as fast as he could back toward the village to tell everyone what he had seen and heard.

On the Mon Lei

“Take her home, Lieutenant Filipov,” boomed Max as he, Kobe, and Alek were bringing the Mon Lei back to BION Island after a short trip sailing the waters around Ripley High.

“Aye, aye, Captain,” said Alek, laughing as he pulled hard on the boat’s wheel to line it up with the dock.

The three RBI agents often enjoyed taking out the boat that had once belonged to the

Ripley High founder, Robert Ripley; and the lovely weather that morning had made this particular trip better than usual.

"Wait till we tell Jack that we saw the bubble-blowing dolphin again," said Kobe. "He'll be desperate to come out here to see it for himself."

"Then he should have come with us," said Max, still slightly put out that his best friend in the RBI had decided to spend the morning in the menagerie tending to the animals, rather than on the water with Max.

"Oops," said Alek as the boat bumped against the dock. "That wasn't my best mooring."

"Anchors away," said Kobe, getting ready to

secure the boat in place. Then he turned to the others. "What did you say?" he asked, his tone suddenly changing.

"I didn't say anything," said Max, getting the sinking feeling that he was about to be accused of having done something bad.

"No, it came from down there," said Kobe, realizing the voice he had heard was not that

of one of his friends.

"It's Mr. Clarkson and Mr. Willis," said Alek.

"Great, my favorite people," groaned Max.

"It doesn't sound as if they are each other's favorite person either," said Kobe. "I think they're arguing. Listen."

The agents pulled themselves down to the deck of the boat and peered through the

railing on the side. This way they could see the discussion, but wouldn't be seen if anyone looked up.

"If we had more security patrolling the halls, there would be less chance of anything getting broken," said Mr. Clarkson. "You know how precious some of the things in the school are."

"Yes, I do," Mr. Willis replied. "But there are just so many better ways that we could spend the extra maintenance budget, Matthew."

"Do you know how much time I spent mending damaged artifacts this term, Shaun?" Mr. Clarkson asked.

"No, but I have a feeling you're going to tell me," Mr. Willis said, sarcastically.

"Hours and hours," Mr. Clarkson complained. "Almost all my time is spent mending, polishing, and cleaning things. There's just so much bad show. Particularly in that corridor with the plaque with the heads on it."

"Isn't that part of a caretaker's job?" asked Mr.

Willis. "Now extra storage would be a good idea. I've bought these new text books—extra thick and absolutely crammed with information on ancient relics and there's just no place for me to keep them. A new storage cupboard would be

perfect and, I think, a much better use of that money. If I can't find room for them soon, I'm going to have to send them back."

"I've seen one of those text books," Max said to the other agents. "It would be much better if they were sent back—they are so boring! Even more boring than the ones he makes us read now!"

"But that corridor that Mr. Clarkson is talking about is where Liu Min is—he means the entrance to the secret RBI lab!"

"I don't think either idea sounds good," said Alek. "The text books we have are bad enough. I don't want any more; and it's hard enough to get into the secret RBI base without more people hanging around. I had to wait for almost 20 minutes the other day to get into the base."

"Do you think any teacher could suggest a way to spend the money?" asked Kobe. "Perhaps we could get Mr. Cain to think of something?"

"Or Dr. Maxwell?" suggested Max. "I bet he could do some wicked stuff to his lab with the extra budget."

Just then all three of the agents' R-phones buzzed with a new message.

"It's a Museum Club message from Mr. Cain," said Alek. Museum Club was the code Mr. Cain used for their RBI messages in case anyone else read the message over their shoulder. "Urgent Museum Club meeting. Come at once, it's going to be 'a mammoth adventure'."

"What do you think it means?" asked Kobe.

Mr. Cain always slipped a clue into the message as to what the agents' next mission would be about.

Alek held a hand up to silence the other two.

"Who's up there?" Mr. Willis shouted. Their R-phones had obviously given away their hiding place and alerted Mr. Willis and Mr. Clarkson that somebody was there.

"Spying on us, are you?" asked Mr. Clarkson.

"Let's see how much they like spying once they're in detention," said Mr. Willis.

"Quickly, this way," said Max pulling the other agents toward the front of the boat. "We should be able to slip through the menagerie and get back into the school building without them noticing us!"

2

Strange Sounds

Alek, Max, and Kobe arrived at the secret RBI base only minutes later, slightly out of breath after their escape from the Mon Lei.

"Text books … hall monitors … no good," Max puffed, obviously more out of breath than the other two.

The rest of the RBI agents who were already gathered in the briefing room looked at him strangely.

"What on earth are you talking about?" asked Kate. "Is it even English?"

"It's American," said Max. "It's an improved version of English." He grinned at Kate as he said it, knowing that it would wind her up.

"I hardly see how it's been improved," she began, rising to the bait.

"Don't start that again," said Jack quickly trying to stop the brewing argument. "Now Max, what did you mean about text books and hall monitors?"

"We heard Mr. Willis and Mr. Clarkson talking," explained Alek.

"Arguing, more like," interrupted Max, who had now caught his breath.

"Really, Mr. Clarkson and Mr. Willis arguing?" asked Jack. "I would like to have seen that!"

"They were ... discussing," said Alek, choosing his words carefully, "the fact that there is some money left in this year's maintenance budget. They were trying to work out how it should be spent."

"Ooh, an auditorium where we could hold concerts would be great," said Li.

"No, an extension to the library would be better," Kate told her. "There just aren't enough good books on the history of language in the Far East. I spent hours trying to find anything on the Teochew dialect from the Guangdong region of China last week."

"Fascinating," said Max sarcastically.

"I was thinking some new equipment for the gym would be a good idea," said Alek. "Perhaps a ski-slope? I've been dying to get more ski-cross experience since I tried it in Aspen with Max last winter."

"And what about Dr. Maxwell?" asked Max. "He could really do with the funds to get some new equipment for his lab, you know."

"You just mean new things you could try out," said Li, smiling.

"Well, yes, but Zia was down there last week

too," said Max "She's bound to have made half of the equipment stop working again. We need to replace so much every time she visits."

Zia decided not to rise to Max's taunting and instead screwed her face up and playfully punched him on the arm.

"Careful, you could have fried my brain with that electric shock," said Max, rubbing his arm and pretending it hurt.

"Only if you had a brain," said Zia smiling.

Kate gave her a high-five for her quick comment.

Max just pulled a face, sulking and knowing that the girls had won.

"Or I could really use a few upgrades, you know," said RIPLEY. All the agents turned as the holographic representation of Robert Ripley appeared above the desk. "With the amount of information in the database these days, some new shortcuts would really save my synapses."

"Stop plotting you lot," said Mr. Cain, smiling as he walked into the RBI lab.

"But Sir, we have to stop Mr. Willis buying more text books," said Max.

"Or Mr. Clarkson from putting more patrols outside the secret lab entrance," Kobe added.

"That might prove tricky," said Mr. Cain. "But there's nothing we can do about it now, I have a mission to brief."

The agents all sat down quietly to listen to Mr. Cain's mission briefing.

"We have received reports of strange things in Tanzania. In the south of the country, not far from the Selous Game Reserve, there have been some weird things happening. Despite the tropical climate of the area a cool, thick fog has gathered off the coast. The fog is then producing a mist that is wafting through a village not far from the coast. That's where our reports have come from."

"Do you think it's like the mist that we

investigated in Japan?" asked Max. "That was actually caused by a large machine."

"I don't think so," said Mr. Cain. "There are other strange things happening in the region too."

The grasses have been trampled, but as far

as anyone knows there are no herds of large animals living in the immediate area."

"Ooh, could it be aliens—like those crop circles that appear in cornfields?" asked Max.

Kate turned and threw him a disapproving look.

"It's always aliens with you, isn't it?" she asked.

"Hey, it could be! We've seen stranger things," Max protested. "When it is aliens, she's going to feel really silly," he added quietly to Jack, who was sitting next to him.

"So these grasses are by the coast?" asked Zia, wanting to get the geography straight in her head. "Like sea grasses?"

"No, the village is not far from the coast, and is just where the land changes to scrubland. There are lots of bushes and grasses before it opens out into the savannah that the area is famous for."

"Ah, I see," said Zia, understanding.

"That's not all," Mr. Cain continued. "There have been sightings of a huge, hairy creature."

"Bigfoot!" shouted Max.

"I don't think Bigfoot is an African legend," said Li.

"There's the Nandi Bear," said Kobe. "It's a very similar legend to Bigfoot. Nandi Bear is described as a large creature, sometimes even as a man, with long, shaggy, reddish-brown fur, who lives in treetops or caves." He turned to Li beside him. "But Nandi Bear is said to be very fond of eating brains!" Kobe ran his hand across Li's head as he said this last bit.

"Gross," said Li, swatting Kobe's hand away.

"Cool!" said Max, referring to both the "brain-eating" reference and to Kobe teasing Li.

"Well the sightings did describe the creature as having long, reddish fur," said Mr. Cain.

"I knew it was Bigfoot, sorry, Nandi Bear," said Max, triumphantly.

"But there is still more," said Mr. Cain. He

indicated RIPLEY, who started an audio file playing.

"What is that?" asked Zia, putting her hands over her ears. "That didn't sound nice."

"It's definitely not a noise I'd expect to hear

in Africa," said Jack.

"It sounded quite prehistoric to me," suggested Li. "Almost like a mammoth or a mastodon."

"Ooh, and they have fur," said Kate, keen to prove this was not some sort of Bigfoot and,

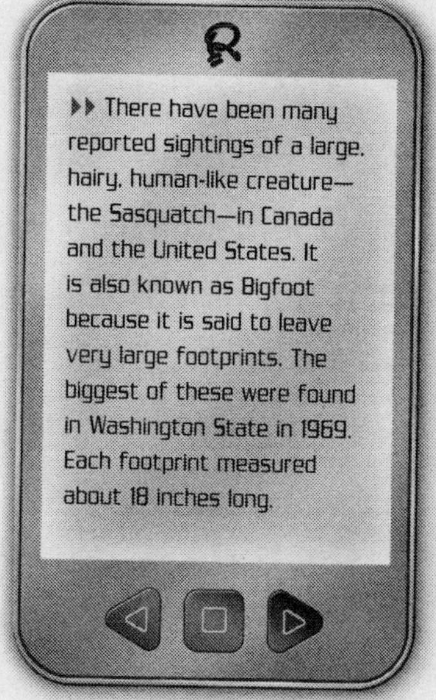

more importantly, prove Max wrong.

"Is it definitely a creature?" asked Kobe.

"If it is, it sounds like it's in pain," said Jack. "Has anyone tried to help it?"

"If I could touch it I might be able to find out more," said Kobe.

"Well you might be able to, as you will be going on the mission," said Mr. Cain. "I was hoping that you might be able to discover something in just that way."

He turned to Jack.

"Jack, obviously you will be going. If there are animals involved your skill set might be needed."

"And if there is an injured animal I want to

be on site to help it," Jack added quickly.

"Also, sound seems to be quite important on this mission," said Mr. Cain, "and we might need someone who can work out exactly what that noise on the audiotape was. So Li, you'll be the third agent."

Li smiled, always happy to be selected to go on missions.

"Great," she said. "I'll go see Miss Burrows and then meet you in Dr. Maxwell's lab."

3

Local Legends

Li arrived at Dr. Maxwell's lab to find Jack, Kobe, and Dr. Maxwell all looking at a table that appeared to have nothing on it.

"What are you doing?" Li asked as she walked over to them. "There's nothing there."

"Ah, but there is," Jack told her.

Dr. Maxwell lifted something from the table and Li saw a small metal airplane.

"Where did that come from?" she asked.

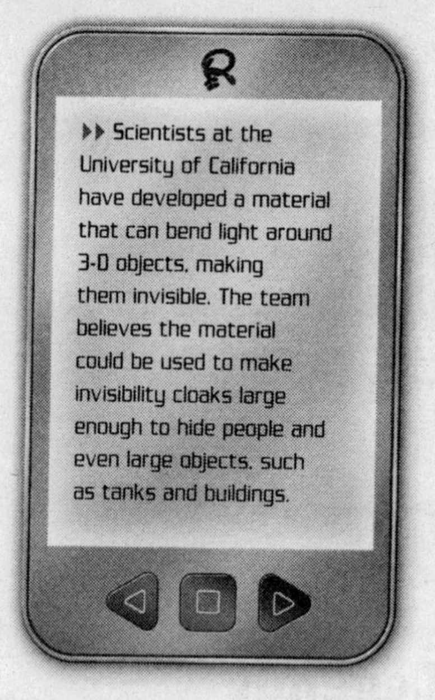

"It's been there all the time," said Dr. Maxwell. "It was just made invisible by this special material." He waved the material in his hand and it glinted and disappeared in patches in the light.

"What is it?" asked Li.

"It's invisibility fabric," Dr. Maxwell explained. "The material bends light and makes it appear as if the object it is covering is not there. I'm currently working on making suits for the RBI out of it."

"That would be so cool," said Kobe.

"I'm not sure Max should be allowed one though," said Li.

"You could be right," said Dr. Maxwell. "I can only imagine the trouble he would get into—

and get me into as well! Anyway you need some gadgets for your mission." As he was putting the material away and rummaging in a store cupboard for something, Kobe turned to Li.

"So what did Miss B. say?" he asked.

"She had quite a lot of information, but I'm not sure how much use it will be," said Li. "She told me that the area I was talking about—the one we will be visiting—is quite near the coast."

"We knew that already," said Jack.

"There's more," Li continued. "She also said that it gets really misty as the sea breeze comes in, particularly in the morning."

"Misty you say?" said Dr. Maxwell, his head appearing from the cupboard.

Li nodded and the doctor disappeared back inside. The agents could hear him searching for something.

"Miss Burrows also started telling me about a local legend," said Li, her voice rising with excitement. "They say that there used to be an island just off the coast, and that if you look at maps from over 100 years ago, you can see it marked there. But the island just vanished. You can't find it on modern maps and as far as anyone knows no one has seen or set foot on the island for over a century. It just disappeared, lost in the mist."

"Woah," said Jack, but before he could comment further, Dr. Maxwell emerged from the cupboard.

"Here you go," he said pulling out a small rectangular box with two prongs on the end.

"Is that a stun gun?" asked Kobe, shocked.

"No, of course not!" said Dr. Maxwell. "It's a visualizer."

"I'll bite," said Li. "What's a visualizer?"

"I was hoping you'd ask!" said Dr. Maxwell, smiling. "It's almost the opposite of the invisibility cloth. It can show you things that are otherwise invisible. It uses the basic form of technology that created RIPLEY," he explained. "It's a very simple hologram projector. The device sends sonic sensors out ahead of itself into, say, mist. Those sonic sensors then feed back to the machine, and then a beam of light connects these two points," he touched the two prongs, "and a very basic hologram of whatever is concealed there will be displayed. Let's try it out. Jack, switch on that smoke machine over there."

Jack walked over to a counter covered with gadgets and found what looked like a-smoke machine. He turned it on and, at once, it started to produce a heavy smoke.

Dr. Maxwell picked up the small airplane and put it in front of the gathering smoke. Soon the agents could no longer see the plane.

"Ready?" asked Dr. Maxwell.

Everyone nodded and Dr. Maxwell turned on the visualizer. It whirred a little and some lights on the screen flashed. Then a small electric charge passed between the two prongs. The power beam, which looked like a tiny bolt of lightning, began to change shape, gradually morphing into something different. The electricity sparked as, slowly, the shape of the plane appeared in the middle of the beam of light.

"That's so cool," said Jack.

"I'm glad you like it," said Dr. Maxwell giving the visualizer to Jack, switching off the smoke

machine, and opening a window to let out the smoke that had already gathered. "Now, Li, this next gadget is for you." Dr. Maxwell handed Li a bright green, hexagonally-shaped gadget with a tiny microphone on the end and a large view-screen.

"Is this some sort of computer game, Sir?" she asked, slightly surprised. "You know I don't really like those things, don't you? Perhaps you should give this to Max."

"Don't worry, it's not a games console," said Dr. Maxwell. "It's a sound sourcer. If you hear any noise—I'm thinking of the strange elephant noise Jack told me about—you need to replicate it exactly for the microphone."

"That won't be a problem for Li," said Kobe. Part of Li's ability was that she could easily copy just about any noise she heard, whether it was natural or not.

"Exactly," said Dr. Maxwell. "When the microphone picks up Li's sound it will search its data banks, which are connected to the main database, and it should be able to tell you what made that noise."

"Cool. Try it out. Do Ziggy the parrot," said Jack. "She makes a really weird noise sometimes if her feathers get in her beak."

Li reproduced the noise made by Ziggy, the bird they referred to as the "feather-duster parrot" due to the fluffy look of her feathers. The sound sourcer took a few seconds as it ran the sound through the database and then an image of Ziggy appeared on the screen with a caption explaining when the parrot had been discovered, a short piece of her history, and that she currently lived at the Ripley High menagerie.

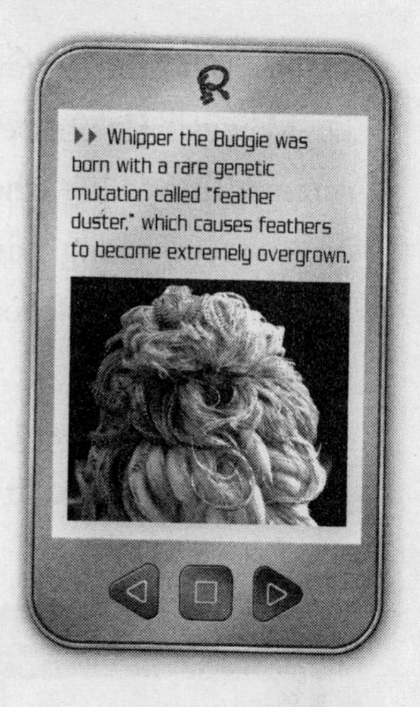

"That's awesome," said Li.

"Now, your final gadget for this mission will be waiting for you over there," Dr. Maxwell told the agents.

"Gadgets that meet us when we arrive are always the best," said Jack, flopping down into a chair in front of the projection screen.

"Then I hope this won't disappoint you," said Dr. Maxwell. He pressed a button and the view screen came to life, showing a large open-top buggy racing along a dirt track.

"Woah, that's so cool," said Jack. "Do we get to drive it?"

"Yes, you do," said Dr. Maxwell throwing some keys to Kobe. "It's an all-terrain vehicle,

or ATV," he explained. "Only when I say 'all-terrain' I mean all-terrain. It's just as good in water as on land, and not just puddles, you can drive through rivers in this."

"How deep a river?" asked Jack with a mischievous look, worthy of Max, on his face.

"Should you need to cross very deep, or very rough, water," said Dr. Maxwell, "there is a little gift in the back. Something that you might find useful."

"That sounds interesting," said Li. "Tell us more."

"If I told you more then it wouldn't be a surprise," said Dr. Maxwell. "Just know that it is one of my own inventions."

"You're the best, Dr. Maxwell," said Kobe, carefully putting the keys in his pocket.

"Right, well no time to waste, you're leaving right away," said Dr. Maxwell, ushering the agents out of his lab.

Noises in the Night

It took the agents just over half a day to reach Tanzania. However, once they had actually arrived, getting around was less easy.

"I'm filthy," complained Li as they stepped off a local bus. She wiped her face to remove the dust that had blown in through the windowless bus they had been riding in. "I've got dirt lines from where my sunglasses have been!" she complained as she looked at her reflection in the bus shelter.

"We're at the coordinates Dr. Maxwell gave us," said Jack. "This is where he told us we should get off."

"Local transport can be slow," said Kobe, "but it is a great way to experience life as the people who live here do."

"But now I've had enough of local transport," said Jack, looking at the ATV that was just ahead of them. "Now I know why Dr. M. wanted us to stop here."

"It's Dr. Maxwell's buggy," said Li.

"Not just a buggy, this is a four-wheel-drive, river-crossing, engine-roaring beast of a thing," said Jack in awe. "And Max is going to be so jealous!" Jack jumped up into the driver's seat.

"He'll be more jealous of me as I'm the one who gets to drive it," said Kobe smiling. He jumped in next to Jack and pushed him along, so that now Kobe was sitting in the driver's seat.

"You two are terrible," said Li pulling herself into the ATV. "I just hope that less dirt gets on me in this than it did on that bus."

"So, where are we going?" asked Jack, turning to Kobe with a mischievous grin. "You're the driver, you have to decide!"

"I thought we'd start at the village where the strange noise was recorded," said Kobe. "See who we can talk to and find out what they know."

"Sounds good," said Li, as Kobe started the engine and the ATV bumped along the rough roads until it reached the small village.

They were greeted by Mosi, the young boy who had sent the audiotape to RIPLEY.

"I am so glad someone came," said Mosi. "These strange noises and things that people have been seeing have frightened some of the villagers."

"Tell us what has happened," said Kobe.

Mosi told the agents about the noise he

RBI

had heard and taped, and how he had seen a great hairy creature and thought that it must have been what made the noises. Since then, he told them, there had been many other strange and horrible sounds coming from inside the fog just off the coast, particularly at night and early in the morning. Other people had seen the strange furry creature, but no one wanted to stick around to see if they could find out what it was.

"It was certainly big, and not like anything I have ever seen before," said Mosi. "Some of the people in my village think it is an angry god come to punish us. I am not sure about that, but it has been damaging our plants and crops, and the idea that it might trample our whole village during the night seems possible."

"Can we speak to some of the other villagers?" asked Kobe. "It's starting to get dark, so we will explore the area and look for strange animals tomorrow morning when it gets light."

"Yes, tonight you should stay here and listen to the noises in the mist," said Mosi. "You can stay in my brother's house. He has gone to Dodoma, our capital city, for work, so his house is empty and I am looking after it."

The RBI agents were made to feel very welcome by Mosi's village. Everyone gathered for a big meal in the village schoolhouse, which they also used for community gatherings. The agents were able to speak to a large number of people. Not everyone spoke English, but Mosi was able to translate, and the agents could recognize the fear and confusion that lots of them, particularly the older generation, felt.

It was very late by the time the agents left the schoolhouse and walked to the small single-story house that Mosi had shown them earlier that evening. As soon as they stepped outside into the night air, they could tell there had been a change in the atmosphere. The air was still warm, but there was a distinct chill to it that seemed to have nothing to do with temperature.

"It's the mist coming in off the sea," said Jack. "There's something strange about it."

"Wait," said Li, turning to the others. "What was that?"

A noise, like the one RIPLEY had played them in the lab, echoed through the mist, but,

in reality, it seemed a lot more menacing.

"Ooh, that sent a shiver right through me," said Li, rubbing her arms. "What is that noise?" She put her hands over her ears.

"It's horrible," she complained, "and that is not the same noise that we heard in the lab."

"Use your sound sourcer," suggested Jack. "I don't think that's any animal noise that I've ever heard. Maybe Dr. Maxwell's device can tell us what is making those noises."

Li pulled the sound sourcer out of her pocket and held it in the direction the sounds were coming from.

It reported back "Error—insufficient sound sample."

"Dr. Maxwell said you should reproduce the noise," Kobe reminded her.

Li copied the noise, with her mouth close to the microphone. This time the machine took a little longer, while it accessed the database and cross-referenced the noises. It came back with

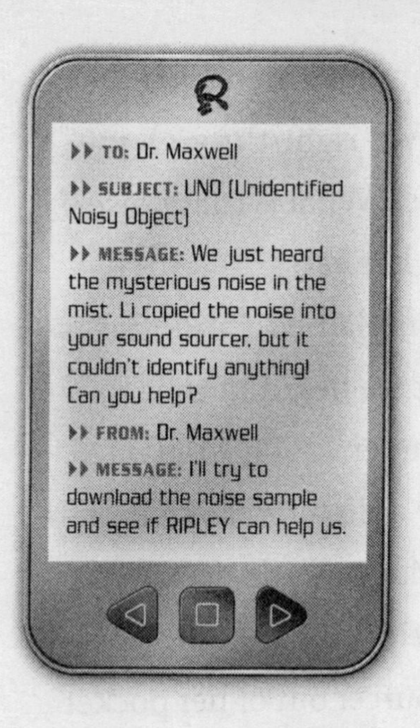

another message: "Error—sound undetermined."

"I must have copied it wrong," said Li. "It sounded different today than it did in the lab."

Kobe and Jack looked at each other, unsure. Li never got sounds wrong. Her pitch-perfect hearing meant that she could reproduce any sound after hearing it only once.

"That really didn't sound like any animal I know," added Jack. "I think that first thing in the morning we just have to set out to solve this mystery, once and for all."

"Sounds good to me!" agreed Kobe.

The next morning the agents woke early. The

sun was streaming in through the windows and the mist from the night before had disappeared.

"Right, let's get going," said Jack to the others, as he pulled on his jacket.

"Woah, you need to see this," said Kobe, as he stepped out the front door.

The area outside the house they had been staying in, all the way back to the main village and the schoolhouse, had been flattened. Every plant and bush in the area had been trampled.

"What on earth happened here?" asked Jack.

"Could an animal have done this?" asked Li stunned at the scene of destruction in front of her.

"Either a lot of animals, or one very scared animal," Jack told her.

Li looked at the crushed grass and plants in amazement. "So is this another mystery, or part of the same one?"

As if in answer, the strange noise that the agents had heard back in the RBI lab sounded

from not too far away.

"Let's find out," said Jack, running in the direction of the noise.

Kobe and Li quickly followed. They caught up with Jack, who was standing still, listening.

"Which way is it, Li?" he asked.

The sound came again, and straightaway Li was able to tell which direction the noise had come from.

Instantly, Jack took off after the noise. The other two ran as fast as they could after him.

Jack stopped behind a large bush to wait for them.

"I think whatever is making the noise is just in this next clearing," he told them. A large grin broke out across his face. "Ready to find out what it is?"

The other agents nodded and Jack pulled back the bushes for them to step through.

In front of them was a huge wall of reddish-brown fur.

'What is that?" asked Li, staring at the amazing sight in front of her, her voice almost a whisper.

5

A Broken Bridge

The creature once again made the noise that they had first heard in Mr. Cain's briefing room.

"It's worse up close," Li complained, clamping her hands over her ears. She watched nervously as Jack approached the beast.

Slowly moving toward the creature, Jack used his ability to soothe it to allow him to approach. He smoothed the long, matted fur and slowly moved around the creature, until he was standing in front of it.

"Amazing," said Jack. "Come and see this."

The other agents slowly and cautiously approached Jack and the creature.

"Is it an elephant?" asked Li.

"I think it's an elephant, of sorts," said Jack looking at the large animal in front of him.

Under the long fur, the creature looked very

much like an African elephant. Except that this elephant had two trunks.

"Why is it like this, then?" asked Li, gesturing to the fur and the extra trunk.

"I've no idea," said Jack. "But isn't it amazing?" he turned to Kobe. "See if you can find out anything about it."

Kobe moved closer to the animal, his hand outstretched ready to touch the creature and hopefully receive flashes of its past, and possibly even its parents, when the elephant suddenly bucked.

The agents hastily stepped back, avoiding the wildly thrashing front legs as the elephant reared onto its hind legs. The amazing noise sounded again

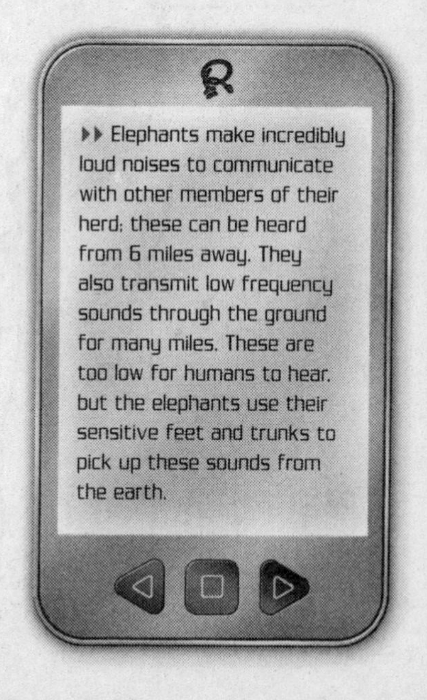

as the elephant cried out.

"What's wrong with it?" asked Li, using her arms as a shield.

"I'm not sure," said Jack, trying to work out a way to calm the animal, but before he could do anything the elephant charged off, through the bushes and toward the open savannah.

The RBI agents ran after it.

"Shouldn't we let it calm down first?" asked Li.

"I'm worried that it's hurt somehow," said Jack. "If that's the case, I want to help it."

"We should get the ATV," said Kobe, gesturing to their truck.

Jack nodded and changed direction, heading toward the ATV.

"Wait," said Li. "I'll go and get it, while you two stay here and keep an eye on the elephant." The two boys watched as Li ran off into the distance, back toward their ATV.

She soon appeared back, with the ATV

bouncing along through the scrubland, and Kobe and Jack jumped in quickly as she stopped for them.

"The elephant ran that way," said Jack. "But we lost sight of it, we just couldn't keep up on foot."

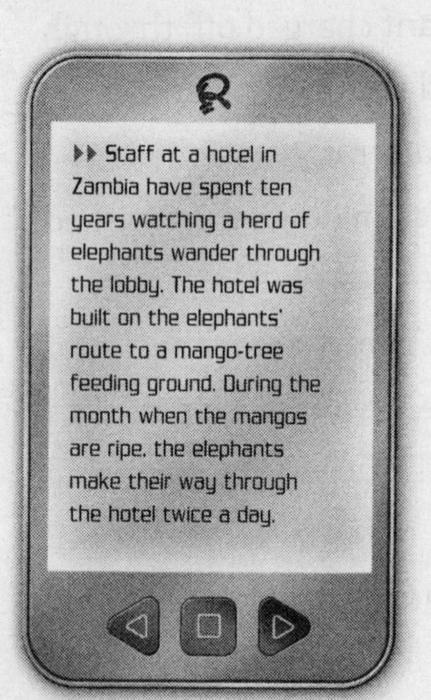

"We'll catch up to it in no time," said Li, the ATV's engine roaring as she hurried it along.

They drove after the elephant, following the path of crushed grass and bushes it left in its wake, and soon they saw it in the distance. As it came clearly into view, the agents saw the creature stumble to its knees.

"It is hurt," said Jack, readying himself to

jump out of the car when they reached the elephant.

But before they got there another vehicle appeared—a large truck.

"Poachers," said Jack, anger sounding in his voice. "They must have shot the elephant with something. Li, drive faster."

Li stepped on the gas pedal and the ATV whizzed forward at top speed.

"Wait, not poachers," said Kobe as he saw some figures pulling the elephant into the back of the truck. He studied their outfits, noting their matching shiny shoes and black sunglasses, and knew that no normal poachers would wear something like that. "DUL agents!"

"They're putting the elephant in their truck," said Li. "What would DUL want with it?"

"What do DUL ever want with anything?" Kobe asked in return. "They must have found out what we were investigating and somehow got here before us, just to stop us from getting a new entry for the database."

"They don't care about the elephant at all," said Jack. "I bet they'll just lock it in a cage somewhere to stop us finding it. We have to stop them."

"I'm on it," said Li, revving the ATV and chasing the DUL agents' truck.

"Be careful," Jack told her, "there are lots of animals that make this area their home, we have to make sure that we don't destroy any habitats, or hurt any animals."

"Tell that to the DUL agents," said Li.

The huge DUL truck was carelessly plowing through trees and bushes. A herd of gazelle leaped quickly out of the way, almost crushed by the large vehicle that was being driven so recklessly. Li had to slow down as the gazelle galloped past her, scattering and trying to escape the action.

"More reason to catch up with them quickly," said Jack.

Li swerved to the left as a large tree branch swung just above their heads. The DUL truck had uprooted the tree it belonged to.

“They are making me really mad,” said Jack, anger obvious in his voice.

“Wait, what’s that?” asked Li.

The DUL truck’s engine was very loud, but Li’s sensitive hearing had picked up something else.

“I can feel it through the floor as well,” she added. “It feels as if the earth is almost shaking.”

“Uh oh,” said Jack.

“What?” asked Li, slightly panicked at Jack’s tone. “What’s wrong?”

“I think it might be a stampede,” Jack explained.

A cloud of dust appeared on the horizon in front of the DUL truck, and the sound of hooves that was making the ground shake grew louder.

“What are they?” asked Kobe, straining to

see through the dust cloud.

"Wildebeest," said Jack. "They must have been scared by the DUL truck."

The herd of wildebeest ran toward the DUL truck and the following RBI ATV.

"What do I do?" asked Li, grimacing as they drove straight into the stampeding herd.

"Keep driving after DUL," said Jack, "but just

be aware that the wildebeest are there."

"Easy for you to say!" Li quickly swerved to avoid the first animal who had almost run right into the side of their ATV.

Li was concentrating on picking a safe path, but there were so many animals it was very difficult.

"Woah!" she shouted as she yanked the wheel hard left, changing course at the last minute to

avoid a wildebeest that had veered in front of the ATV.

"DUL will have to slow down to get through this too," said Jack, watching as the huge DUL truck began to slow, jerking dangerously as it tried to move out of the path of the charging wildebeest.

"They're heading toward that bridge," said Kobe, pointing to an old rickety-looking wooden bridge that crossed a wide river.

"That bridge doesn't look like it's going to hold their truck," said Li.

"I don't think it was built to carry anything quite so heavy," said Kobe.

The RBI agents watched as the DUL transport vehicle carefully drove onto the wooden bridge, which creaked and groaned under its weight. Li stopped their ATV near the edge of the river to watch. Part of the DUL plan was working as the wildebeest didn't follow their truck toward the bridge, but instead ran off in the opposite direction, back into the bushes. But it left the heavy truck dangerously balanced on a very fragile bridge.

The planks of wood that made up the old bridge started to move, groaning loudly under the weight of the heavy vehicle and the added weight of the elephant inside it.

"It's going to give way!" said Jack, realizing what was happening, "And the elephant is still in the back, knocked out by that dart!"

He started to leap out of the ATV, when a trunk appeared out of the back of the DUL truck and then another, and the loud, unusual, elephant call carried through the air toward them.

"I think the elephant is awake," said Li.

The DUL truck began to drop down into the water and all around them planks started to snap and shatter. The DUL agents quickly jumped out of the sinking truck and ran or swam to the shore as fast as they could, then disappeared into the undergrowth.

The elephant in the back called out loudly.

"Just like DUL agents to leave the elephant there," said Jack, out of the ATV and ready to jump into the water to help the stranded elephant.

"I don't think we need to worry," said Kobe.

The elephant had pulled itself out the back of the DUL truck, which was now almost completely immersed in the river, and had begun swimming to the river bank.

"She's a strong swimmer," commented Jack as he ran to meet the elephant when it reached the riverside.

6

Echoes

The elephant was still nervous after being shot with the tranquilizer dart by the DUL agents, and Jack couldn't blame it. He approached the creature slowly and, using his ability, gradually calmed it down until it allowed him to move right up beside it. Jack gently placed a hand on the elephant's side, all the time whispering reassuringly to the giant creature.

"Where did you come from?" Jack asked. He

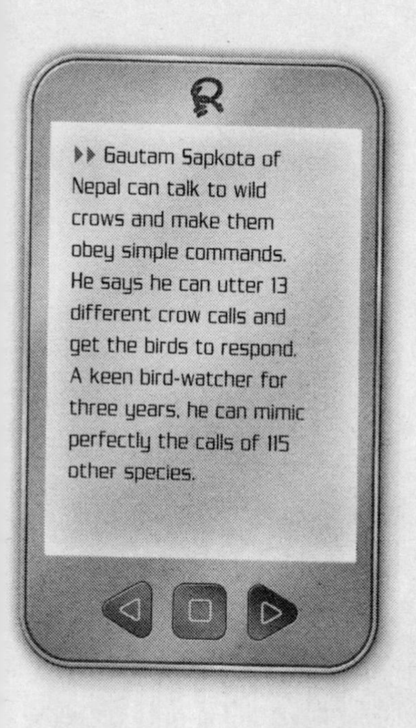

turned to the other RBI agents. "Kobe?" he called. "Can you help here?"

Kobe began to walk slowly toward Jack and the elephant. Cautiously placing a hand on the elephant, Kobe was able to use his ability to sense things that had happened to the creature.

He saw the elephant running free in what he thought might be a large safari park; then the images changed and he was seeing flashes of other creatures too, but couldn't quite identify them, the visions were moving too fast. Kobe pulled his hand away and turned toward the other agents.

"I couldn't see clearly where the elephant

comes from," said Kobe. "But it didn't seem as if it was from here."

As he told the others about the things he had seen, the elephant seemed to grow restless. It began to move, quite slowly, but purposefully, walking through the savannah.

"We should follow it," said Li, beginning to move after the elephant.

"Let's take the ATV," said Jack.

The agents tracked the elephant, following it in their ATV, until it reached the coastline, where it stopped and stared out into the distance at the thick fog gathering over the water.

"What's it doing?" asked Kobe as he got out of the ATV.

The elephant began calling out.

The agents watched it for a moment and then were amazed as they heard a faint echo in reply.

"Is there something out there bouncing the sound back?" asked Kobe.

"No, it didn't sound quite like an echo," said Li. "The tone was slightly different. I think something else made that noise."

"Like what?" asked Kobe.

"Perhaps there's another elephant out there," said Jack.

Kobe took the visualizer that Dr. Maxwell had given him from his bag and switched it on, pointing it toward the mist.

The beam of light between the electrodes pulsed and glowed, but nothing appeared.

"The fog must be too thick to pick out anything," said Kobe.

The elephant called again but before the second call sounded in the distance, the agents heard voices: people shouting anxiously for the elephant to be quiet.

They walked along the shoreline to a patch where the fog had covered the edge of the land, and found a group of three fishermen, standing in the shallows, their fishing rods disappearing into the thick mist just off the shore.

The RBI agents introduced themselves to the fishermen, who looked terrified.

"What is that weird beast making that horrible noise?" one of them asked, his hands on the fishing rod shaking with fear.

"It's an elephant," said Li, "a slightly strange-looking elephant, but it seems to be friendly and it's calling into the mist. Do you know what is out there?"

"There's nothing good out there," said the first fisherman.

"And nothing that goes out there ever comes back," said the second.

"I heard that the same thing that makes the

fish bigger here makes the water dangerous," said the third fisherman. "People tell stories about fishermen who got greedy and decided to go out into the mist to see if the fish got even bigger out there. Only no one ever found out if the fish were bigger, because none of them ever returned."

"What do you mean, 'never returned'?" asked Kobe.

"Just that. They never came back," said the fisherman. "No one knows what happened to them. They must still be out there, lost in the mist."

Li looked out into the mist and gulped. She didn't much like the idea of being lost in it forever.

"But those are just legends, surely," said Kobe.

"I don't know; there are a lot of stories like that. Everyone knows someone whose friend disappeared," said the fisherman.

"But no one knows any names?" asked Kobe. "That's how urban legends form."

The fishermen shook their heads.

"Can't think of any," one said.

"Whatever is out there in that mist, it must be pretty special to encourage so many stories about it," Kobe said turning to the other agents. "I think we need to go investigate."

"It's going to be an exciting adventure," said Jack as the elephant called out loudly again. The second call sounded through the mist, once more, and the elephant stepped off the shore and began to disappear into the eerie fog.

Into the Mist

"It looks like the elephant has started its mission without us," said Kobe, as the creature began swimming out of sight in the thick fog.

"We'd better catch up quickly," suggested Jack, starting to run toward the ATV.

"You can't use that," said one of the fishermen. The water's very deep just off the shore and there are some really strong currents."

"Didn't Dr. Maxwell say that there was

something else in the back that we could use in deep water?" asked Li.

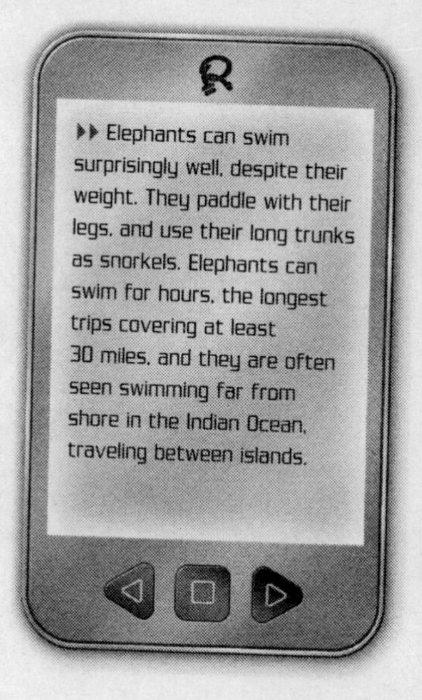

"You're right," said Jack, racing around to the back of the ATV. He pulled out a strange, futuristic-looking box, which looked almost like a metal egg. On it was a note on in Dr. Maxwell's handwriting that read "Your surprise." He carried the small box around to the others before opening it. As he did, a huge swell of yellow material rocketed out. The material kept growing and the agents had to step back as it filled the area around them. When it stopped expanding, the agents saw that it was, in fact, a lightweight speedboat, and the egg-shaped box was a small motor that now sat on the back of the boat.

"Wow, that's amazing," said Kobe. "How did that big boat fit into that tiny box?"

"I think the military use things like this," said Jack. "They are very hard-wearing boats, but they fold up small so they can be taken around the world really easily."

"I wonder if they could make a suitcase where everything folds in that small?" said Li. "I could take so much more on missions!"

"We'd better hurry and get this in the water," said Jack.

The elephant was almost invisible as the agents lowered the incredibly light boat into the water. The elephant was vanishing into the distance, getting swallowed up by the mist.

The water started off quite calm, but soon the currents began to gain strength and it became harder to steer the boat.

"The elephant seems to be picking the safest and easiest route through," Jack told the others as another wave washed over the small speedboat, drenching the agents in salty seawater.

"Watch out!" shouted Kobe. Even though they were following the elephant it was hard going. A huge wave appeared and the agents had to hold on tightly as the boat was rocked violently, almost flipping over.

"I thought we were going under then," said Li, pulling her soaking hair away from her face. "What was that?"

"I don't know, but I think it was more than just a normal wave," said Jack.

"Wait, where's the elephant gone?" asked Kobe, suddenly alarmed.

The agents looked around and couldn't see any sign of the elephant.

"Ooh, is that it under the water?" asked Li, pointing at a large shape that had appeared

very close to their boat.

"No," said Kobe slowly, straining due to the fog to see the shape. "I don't think that is an elephant. It looks far too big."

"What is it then?" said Li trying to keep the fear from her voice.

"I'm not really sure," said Jack.

Suddenly the speedboat started to shake.

"What ever it is is right under us," said Jack,

"and I think it's trying to tip us over."

"How do we make it stop?" asked Li.

"It must be some sort of whale," said Jack, trying to stay calm. "I don't think there are many whales that are native to this area, and definitely not any that would be this close to land, but I can't think of any other explanation."

"Maybe whatever it is is what made those people the fishermen knew disappear," said Li, trying to hide her rising fear.

"No, it must be some sort of animal," said Jack reassuringly, "and if it's an animal I should be able to calm it down and hopefully move it away from the boat."

"You'd better do something quickly," said Li as the creature jolted the speedboat again, sending it tumbling so that it only just remained the right way up.

"I'm going to go into the water and see what I can do," Jack told them. He was trying to sound brave and convince himself and the others that it would just be a whale that had got lost, but his voice wavered as he struggled to think calmly. Jack was normally one of the bravest RBI agents, but the idea of diving into the water with something that cast a shadow of that size would worry even the most heroic person.

"Be careful," Li told him, not sure it was a good idea for Jack to jump in with the monstrous creature threatening to capsize them, but knowing that if he didn't they might not make it back to land.

Jack looked back at them both and then dove into the water.

Only seconds after Jack jumped overboard, the water began to calm until it became eerily still.

"What's happened?" asked Li. "I can hardly see any ripples at all on the water now."

"I know," agreed Kobe. "But where's Jack?"

8

Prehistoric Problems

Suddenly a huge shape broke the surface of the water, jumping into the air. Its back arched gracefully as it bowed like a rainbow and began to dive back down. As its head disappeared back beneath the dark water an enormous tail appeared behind it. Flicking powerfully as it followed the rest of the creature, it sent a giant splash and huge ripples out toward Kobe and Li in their boat.

They clutched the strong, rubbery sides once more, as the waves rocked their speedboat.

"What was that thing?" asked Li, more to herself than Kobe.

Then a smaller splash appeared and, to the shocked agents' relief, Jack's head broke the surface.

"Wow, did you guys see that?" he asked, his voice filled with excitement. "I mean, did you

see that thing? It's incredible!"

He pulled himself toward the speedboat and clambered up over the side, shaking out his hair in the way a wet dog might do.

Li grimaced as water splashed all over her.

"Incredible," Jack said again.

"So what is it?" asked Li, brushing the water off her clothes.

"Well, I'm not entirely sure," Jack told her.

I took a picture of it using the R-phone's underwater camera and have sent it back to the RBI base to get them to double-check for me, but I think it's some type of prehistoric creature.

"Wait, prehistoric?" asked Kobe, sounding unconvinced.

"I know," said Jack. "I'm not sure I believe it either, which is why I want Kate to take a look at it. But I can't think of anything else it could possibly be!"

"What about a blue whale?" asked Li. "They're

pretty big."

"In fact, they're bigger than that thing," said Jack.

His R-phone beeped loudly and he quickly started scrolling through the message.

"Yes!" he shouted. "It is a prehistoric creature!" He leaped to his feet. "We are the first people to see something that everyone has thought to be extinct for millions of years!"

▸▸ SENDER: Kate
▸▸ SUBJECT:
Found this story in the database. Is this what you saw?
▸▸ MESSAGE: Norwegian scientists have discovered the existence of a huge prehistoric sea reptile that measured 50 feet long. The 150-million-year-old plesiosaur would have been able to pick up a small car in its jaws and bite it in half.

"But what's it doing here?" asked Li. "Wait, what was that?" she asked before anyone could answer her first question.

Kobe strained and he could hear what had caught Li's attention too. It was the elephant.

"We could catch up to it easily," said Kobe.

Still buzzing from his encounter with the prehistoric reptile, Jack took over steering the motor boat and they sped off in the direction of the elephant, moving carefully through the fog.

"Where's the elephant taking us?" asked Li, once they had caught up with the creature and were following its path through the water. "It must be going somewhere." She tried to stare through the mist and see what might be out there.

"Let me try the visualizer again," suggested Kobe. He pulled the gadget out of his pocket and switched it on.

The energy beam pulsed between the two electrodes as it had done before, but this time it began to move more energetically, before it took on a shape.

The beam gave the agents a rough impression of a rocky island.

"Wow," said Li. "I wonder if that's the island

Miss Burrows told me about. The one that disappeared from maps."

"It seems to have disappeared altogether in this fog," said Kobe. "If we can see it on the visualizer we can't be very far away now."

"Eugh, what is that awful smell?" asked Li.

"I think it's coming from the water," said Kobe. "There must be some sort of gas in it, like sulfur. That smells like rotten eggs."

"Whatever it is, it's getting stronger," said Li, putting a handkerchief over her nose and mouth, trying to block the smell.

"The fog is getting thicker, too" said Kobe. "I can hardly see the elephant now."

"We'll just have to follow its calls," said Jack. "Li, I might need your help to pinpoint the direction."

Li nodded, her hanky still over her nose.

"Look at the water," said Kobe, pointing.

Because the mist was so thick, the agents could only see the water right next to their boat, and it had just started to bubble.

Kobe held his hand over the side, close to the surface.

"It's not hot," he said. "So it can't be boiling. There must be some sort of natural gas in this area."

"Could the gas be linked to a volcano?" asked Jack.

"It could be," said Kobe.

Jack pointed, and as Kobe looked, the fog started to clear and a large mountain peak emerged before them, surrounded by tropical forest.

"Wow, are we there?" asked Li.

"Thanks to the elephant," said Jack. "I don't think we would have been able to find our way

▸▸ Giulia Ferdinanda, a tiny volcanic island off the coast of Sicily, Italy, regularly emerges from, and disappears under, the waves of the Mediterranean Sea.

▸▸ Vulcan Island, in Rabaul harbor, Papua New Guinea, rose from the ocean floor in a single night in 1870. Within a few years, the volcano had grown to become a 590-foot peak.

through that mist without its help."

"That must be why no one has found this island for so long," said Kobe. "That and the prehistoric monster, of course, which would have sunk us if it wasn't for you, Jack."

As the boat drew closer, the agents could see an island sprawling around the huge mountain peak, which was sending a neat plume of smoke billowing up into the air around it.

"It looks like an active volcano," said Jack.

"Do you think it's safe to step into the water?" asked Li, looking down at the still bubbling liquid.

"I'd say we can stand in it quickly," said Kobe. "I just suggest that we don't stay in it for too long."

"And it hasn't affected the elephant," said Jack pointing to the elephant who was lumbering along beside them.

All three agents stepped out of the boat, and moved quickly through the fizzing water and across a small beach, which was quite unusual, as all the sand was black.

"The sand is made from lava rock," said Li as she walked across the volcanic beach. She stepped onto the lush green floor on the island, following the elephant who had waded ashore before them.

As soon as they began walking, the RBI agents

realized that they weren't alone on this island. They could hear the rustling of creatures in the bushes and grass all around them, and strange bird calls sounded in the trees and the sky above.

"It sounds like there are thousands of birds here," said Li.

"I don't recognize many of the calls though," said Jack. "Some of them sound like people talking."

Li stepped on a twig, which snapped under her foot. Immediately a large flock of birds took flight out of a nearby bush, their flapping wings making even more noise. She jumped back and gasped with surprise.

Kobe and Jack were both laughing at her.

The agents were pleased that the elephant was leading the way for them. Although the sun was bright, in places the trees formed a canopy overhead and blocked out most of the light, sometimes making it hard to see.

Eventually they came to a rise above a large clearing, where the elephant stopped.

There were patches of wispy mist in the clearing that, strangely, didn't seem to be on the areas of the island they had walked through. The mist was not thick enough to stop the agents from making out what was happening below them; they could see large trucks and men struggling with animals.

"DUL agents," said Kobe. "But what are they doing?"

As they watched, the agents were dragging animals into the clearing, many of them tied awkwardly with ropes, and then trying to wrestle the animals into large trucks.

"Is that a dodo?" asked Jack in awe. He fished around in his bag for a pair of binoculars to get a better look. "It, is!" he exclaimed. "It really is. This is so amazing!"

9

Mysterious Island

Jack continued to look at all the animals, picking out a number that were different or were thought to have been extinct.

"What are DUL doing with them?" asked Kobe, "And more importantly, how do we stop them."

"The animals don't seem to be scared of humans," said Jack. "They appear to be quite happy to go with the DUL agents until they try to put them into the trucks."

The elephant started calling loudly, and the echoing call they had heard on the African shore came back, louder now.

Jack moved the binoculars to find the source of the call.

"There's another elephant, just like ours," said Jack.

"This one came back for his friend," said Li.

The other elephant struggled more forcefully, hearing the call of its mate.

"That gives me an idea," said Jack. "The animals might not be scared of humans, but how about a large predator? Li, could you make the noise of a lion?"

Li nodded and produced, perfectly, the sound

of an angry, hungry lion which echoed across the valley below them.

Many of the animals began to struggle, breaking the ropes holding them and pulling away from the DUL agents. Then they started to stampede, keen to escape. The DUL agents ran in every direction to avoid the startled animals.

"Yeah! The animals are free," said Jack, happily.

"Shh," said Li. "I can hear someone coming."

"It must be one of the DUL agents," said Kobe.

The agents moved back into one of the thick, green bushes and stood there silently. As the approaching footsteps grew louder Jack leaped out and grabbed the person by the arm.

"What are you doing with those animals?" Jack shouted, only to find that the arm he was holding didn't belong to a DUL agent at all, but to a woman, with shoulder-length, dark

hair, wearing safari clothing. "Who are you?" asked Jack.

"I work on the island," she told them. "I've been watching those men in the clearing, trying to think of a good way to get rid of them. It's my fault they are here."

"You work here?" asked Jack, suspiciously.

"And what do you mean it's your fault they are here?"

The woman explained to them that her name was Dr. Leanne Hartley and she was a scientist. She had always studied animals, and had found this island while on a trip around the African coast. It hadn't been on any maps and there had been no directions to it, so she mapped its location herself, so she could return whenever she wanted. She was amazed at the rich biodiversity on the island; it suited her work perfectly.

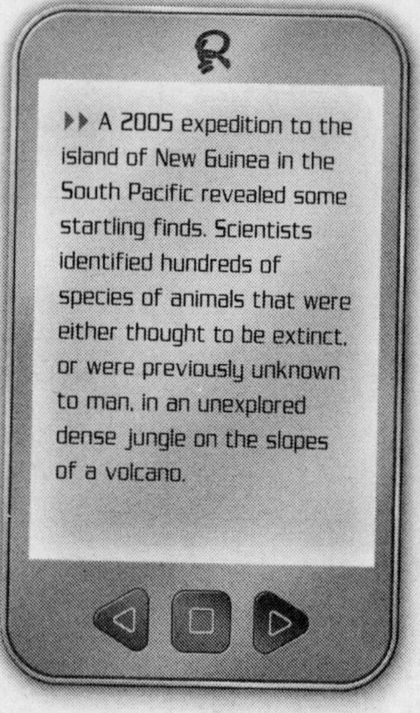

Not only were there an amazing number of plants and animals that had been left to flourish without man's interference, but a large portion of the wildlife had developed in different ways to that which you normally see.

"There were plants with flowers as big as monster truck wheels," she explained, "beautiful, intense blooms that gave off the sweetest smells. There were trees that I had seen nowhere in the world before and some that I had thought extinct. And then there were the animals." She paused and looked at the agents. "For some reason, lots of the animals had genetic anomalies; birds with larger than normal wingspans, elephants with extra trunks and shaggy hair, and nocturnal creatures happy to come out during the day. I knew there was something special about this island. Not only that, but, most incredible of all, there were lots of creatures that had been thought to be extinct for millions of years." She pointed to a large tree on the far side of the island, but visible due to its size. "There's a family of pteranodons that live in that big tree over there."

"Wow," said Li, genuinely impressed. "You know so much about this place."

"It's my home away from home," she told the RBI agents. "If you come with me I'll take you to my house."

"So how did DUL find the island?" asked Kobe as they walked.

Dr. Hartley sighed. "As I said, it was completely my fault. I brought them here."

The Island Fights Back

"A couple of months ago, I received an offer of funding from a company who called themselves the Defence of Uncommon animals League, or DUL. They said that they had heard about the island and my research and wanted to invest a lot of money in me and my animals, but wanted to see the island for themselves before they invested such a huge amount. The money they were offering was amazing. This island is getting too crowded for all of the animals that are on it now, and the funds I would have received meant some of them could have been moved to other places to get better care than I can give them now." Dr. Hartley paused and shook her head. "I just didn't think. I should have known that there was no way this DUL company could have found out about my work. I've kept my trips to the island very secret. When they arrived on the island all they wanted to do was to capture the animals. They had no interest in my work at all."

"We had heard reports of strange things in the area and DUL must have, too," explained Kobe.

"But they met a problem when they tried to catch the two-trunked elephant, who escaped and swam away from the island," said Dr. Hartley.

"But it came back for the other one," said Li.

Dr. Hartley nodded. “They are a pair.”

“What is that?” asked Jack as they stopped in front of a wooden structure built in one of the large trees.

“That’s my ‘hotel’,” said the doctor. She grabbed a long rope ladder and began climbing up it into the branches of the tree.

Kobe followed, then Li and Jack.

“This is incredible!” said Li.

"It was here when I first got to the island," said Dr. Hartley. "It looked like no one had been inside it for years, but once I cleaned it up a bit, it was the perfect place for me to stay."

"Hey guys, look at this," said Kobe as he walked over to a still dusty shelf. He picked up a tin that looked exactly like the one that Li had brought back from Canada.

"It looks like another clue tin!" said Li.

The RBI agents needed to keep a close eye out for tins just like this on their missions. Robert Ripley, founder of the RBI, had left tins like this all over the world with clues concealed inside them. Once the agents had all the clues, they were led to an amazing discovery—last time it had been a crystal skull in the Antarctic.

"That tin was here when I first got to the island," said Leanne.

"May I open it?" asked Kobe.

Leanne nodded and Kobe opened the blue and silver tin. A small coin fell out.

"What's that?" asked Jack.

"It looks like a peso," said Leanne.

"That's the currency they use in Mexico," said Li. "Perhaps it got there by mistake?"

"Or perhaps that is the clue," suggested Jack. "Rip's clues are quite often hard to work out until you have more of them."

"Kate will think of something," said Li. "She's brilliant at problem solving."

"There's one problem we can't rely on Kate for," said Jack. "How to get those DUL agents off the island?"

"Well, I think I know," said Dr. Hartley. "The island has its own defence mechanisms."

The doctor led the agents back to the clearing, where almost all the animals had disappeared, leaving lots of very cross-looking DUL agents and empty trucks.

"See all that mist in the clearing?" asked Dr. Hartley.

All three RBI agents nodded.

"Well, it's the same sort of gas that fills the water. It's not a gas you will have come across," said Dr. Hartley. "It is a mixture of several, but is harmless to breathe and to swim in. It seems to be partly responsible for the unusual animal life here. If you set fire to it, it is also quite flammable."

She walked to the edge of the clearing over to a sink hole that was spewing the misty gas into the area. She pulled a box of matches out of her pocket and struck one, so that the gas immediately began to spark into flame.

She then walked back to the agents and they all watched as the flames began to grow, eating up the gas and rolling toward the DUL agents.

The DUL agents realized what was happening and began shouting to each other.

Jack couldn't help but snigger to himself as

the DUL agents crashed into each other trying to get away.

Once they recovered a little they all ran in the same direction, toward the coast.

Dr. Hartley and the RBI agents followed to see what would happen.

The DUL agents ran right into the sea, to where the large boats they had arrived in were waiting. They started up the boats and shot away into the mist.

"Isn't that fire going to burn down lots of the island?" asked Jack, concerned.

"No, don't worry," said Dr. Hartley. "The fire will feed on the gas in the clearing, but will then burn itself out. I've seen it do that lots of times, when there has been a lightning strike or something else that has set it alight."

"I can't see the DUL agents coming back again now," said Li.

"I don't think they could find the island again without me to guide them", said Dr.

Hartley, "and I have no intention of doing that again!"

"But what about the animals?" asked Jack. "I thought you said that extra funding would have helped you as the island is getting too crowded."

"I'll just have to think of something else," said the doctor.

"Well, I may have an idea," said Jack, a mischievous look playing across his face.

"Oh no, he's got that 'Max' look again," said Li. "That can only mean trouble!"

"We have this menagerie on BION island," explained Jack. "It doesn't have all the natural gases and stuff that this one has, but the animals would be safe there and well looked after."

As Jack spoke the two elephants approached the group. The elephant they had followed began to nuzzle Jack with its two trunks.

"The animals do seem to like you," said Dr.

Hartley, "and it would solve a lot of space issues."

"Then it's settled," said Jack, pulling his R-phone out of his pocket and dialing.

"Wait a minute," said Li. "You are never going to find room in the menagerie for these animals!"

"Oh, don't worry about that," said Jack. "I have a plan. Oh, hello, Mr. Cain is that you?" Jack spoke into the phone as his teacher answered it back at Ripley High. "I think I've found a great way to spend that extra maintenance budget. A new menagerie expansion!"

The others groaned as Jack enthusiastically continued to sell his idea to Mr. Cain.

RIPLEY'S DATABASE ENTRY

RIPLEY FILE NUMBER : 64682

MISSION BRIEF : Believe it or not, strange noises have been heard near the Tanzanian coast along with reports of trampled grass and thick fog. Investigate these accounts for Ripley database.

CODE NAME : Two Trunks

REAL NAME : Elephant-Mammoth

LOCATION : Island off Tanzania

AGE : Unknown

HEIGHT : 11 ft 6 in

WEIGHT : 10 tons

VIDEO CAPTURE

UNUSUAL CHARACTERISTICS :

Looks more like a modern elephant than a woolly mammoth (with normal elephant tusks) but taller, with red shaggy fur, two trunks and a distinctive call, somewhere between a roar and a scream.

INVESTIGATING AGENTS :

Jack Stevens, Kobe Shakur, Li Yong

ENTER THE STRANGE WORLD OF RIPLEY'S ...

Believe it or not, there is a lot of truth in this remarkable tale. The Ripley's team travels the globe to track down true stories that will amaze you. Read on to find out about real Ripley's case files and discover incredible facts about some of the extraordinary people and places in our world.

Ripley's Believe It or Not!®

CASE FILE #001

▶▶ TWO TRUNKS

Ripley's took possession of this preserved head in August 2005—the elephant itself had died in Zimbabwe, Africa, in November 2004.

▶▶ Scientific analysis has found that the two trunks contain identical DNA patterns and that they were definitely from the same animal.

▶▶ Amazingly both trunks functioned at the same time.

▶▶ The head, on its own, weighs about a ton.

▶▶ Animals with more than one face, or facial feature, are examples of the genetic condition diprosopus.

ISLAND DISCOVERIES

MADAGASCAR

▸▸ Madagascar is a large island off the coast of Africa full of rare animals. It is the fourth largest island in the world.

▸▸ Madagascar was home to the biggest bird ever, Aepyornis, which stood 10 feet tall and weighed as much as a horse.

▸▸ With one Aepyornis egg you could make about 50 omelettes but, unfortunately, they died out 400 years ago.

▸▸ Scientists recently reported that they could bring the giant Aepyornis birds back to life by getting DNA from ancient eggs, which are 150 times bigger than regular chicken eggs.

▸▸ In June 2007, scientists found an extremely rare plant that eats rats on a remote island in the Philippines.

▸▸ On the tropical island of Borneo in the Pacific Ocean, more than 400 new species have been found in a rainforest the size of Kansas, USA. The strange creatures include gliding frogs that change color at night, deadly snakes, and stick insects 20 inches long.

CASE FILE #002

▶▶ ZAK-N-WHEEZIE

Frank and Barbara Witte of California, have an unusual pet—a two-headed bearded dragon called Zak-n-Wheezie. Their lizard has two names because it was born with two heads.

▶▶ Experts thought that the lizard would not live for long, but Zak-n-Wheezie is still going strong and is probably the oldest two-headed lizard around.

▶▶ Bearded dragons are born with two heads more often than any other creature.

▶▶ Two-headed dragons have two separate brains, but can often coordinate their bodies surprisingly well.

ELEPHANTS

▸▸ In 1956, an African elephant was found that weighed 12 tons and stood 13 feet high, that's taller than someone standing on another person's head.

▸▸ Elephant trunks can suck up three and a half gallons of water, that's about 40 cans of soda, at once.

▸▸ Elephants live as long as humans. The oldest known elephant lived to at least 80 years old.

▸▸ An elephant can produce a ton of dung in a week, that's about the weight of a car in poo.

▸▸ Elephants can copy the sounds in their environment. In Kenya, Mlaika, a ten-year-old elephant, mimicked the sound of trucks rumbling along a nearby highway.

▸▸ A large African elephant eats more than 450 pounds of food each day—the weight of two large humans—and this is mostly grass.

CASE FILE #003

▶▶ PLESIOSAURS

The plesiosaurs were prehistoric sea reptiles with long necks, stout bodies, and four powerful flippers.

▶▶ Remains have been found of plesiosaurs that were as long as two buses and weighed the same as 15 pick-up trucks. Experts think some may have been even bigger than that.

▶▶ They may have eaten birds as well as fish, and would have used their powerful flippers to launch themselves from the water to take food from the air.

▶▶ The huge size of the plesiosaurs makes them the largest predators ever discovered on Earth.

RIPLEY

In 1918, Robert Ripley became fascinated by strange facts while he was working as a cartoonist at the *New York Globe*. He was passionate about travel and, by 1940, had visited no fewer than 201 countries, gathering artifacts and searching for stories that would be right for his column, which he named Believe It or Not!

Ripley bought an island estate at Mamaroneck, New York, and filled the huge house there with unusual objects and odd creatures that he'd collected on his explorations.

- In his lifetime, Ripley traveled over 450,000 miles looking for oddities—the distance from Earth to the Moon and back again.

- Ripley had a large collection of cars, but he couldn't drive. He also bought a Chinese sailing boat, called Mon Lei, but he couldn't swim.

- Ripley was so popular that his weekly mailbag often exceeded 170,000 letters, all full of weird and wacky suggestions for his cartoon strip.

- He kept a 28-feet-long boa constrictor as a pet in his New York home.

- Ripley's Believe It or Not! cartoon is the longest-running cartoon strip in the world, read in 42 countries and 17 languages every day.

RIPLEY'S
RBI
FACT OR FICTION?
BUREAU OF INVESTIGATION

FUN!

The team fights on for truth and justice in the world of the weird ...

RIPLEY'S
RBI
FACT OR FICTION?
BUREAU OF
INVESTIGATION